Under the Sea
with Googol and Googolplex

Nelly Kazenbroot

ORCA BOOK PUBLISHERS

National Library of Canada Cataloguing in Publication:

Kazenbroot, Nelly, 1960-
Under the sea with Googol and Googolplex / Nelly Kazenbroot.

(Orca echoes)
ISBN 1-55143-366-4

1. Human-alien encounters--Juvenile fiction. 2. Robots--Juvenile fiction.
I. Title. II. Series.

PS8571.A965U53 2005   jC813'.54   C2004-907239-0

Library of Congress Control Number: 2004117321

Summary: Alien robots Googol and Googolplex are back to continue their scavenger hunt
in this sequel to *Down the Chimney with Googol and Googolplex*.

Orca Book Publishers gratefully acknowledges the support for its
publishing programs provided by the following agencies: the Government of Canada
through the Department of Canadian Heritage's Book Publishing Industry Development
Program (BPIDP), the Canada Council for the Arts, and the British Columbia Arts Council.

Design and typesetting: Lynn O'Rourke

Orca Book Publishers
Box 5626 Stn. B
Victoria, BC Canada
V8R 6S4

Orca Book Publishers
PO Box 468
Custer, WA USA
98240-0468

Printed and bound in Canada

08 07 06 05 • 4 3 2 1

To Marvin the Martian,
an old friend of Googol and Googolplex.
—N.K.

Chapter One
Old Friends

The round Earth is a confusing place for a couple of square-headed robots from outer space. But Googol and Googolplex have been here once before. This time, they know where they are going. They have come to visit their friends, Troy and Pippa Sinclair.

Googol points down at a nice red house with lots of square windows and a triangular roof.

"There it is!" Googolplex says. His head spins around three times.

"Perfect!" Googol says.

They bring their spaceship down out of the blue summer sky.

Pippa and Troy are in the backyard.

They are standing beside a large inflatable pool. They are having trouble deciding who gets to jump in first. Troy pumped up the pool, but Pippa filled it with water.

"Why don't we jump in at the same time?" Troy says.

"All right," Pippa says.

She stands on one side of the pool, and Troy stands on the other. Pippa is six years old, and Troy is eight, and the pool is just the right size for both of them.

"One, two, three, go!" Troy calls out.

There is a big splash as they both jump in. When they finally stop laughing and splashing about, they look up into the air.

Googol and Googolplex's spaceship makes a soft, buzzing noise and it is invisible to humans. Pippa thinks a bee is flying around them. She waves her hands to shoo it away.

Troy stands up in the pool. The buzzing stops. He smiles.

"It's not a bee, silly. Look!" he says.

Pippa turns her head just in time to see Googol and Googolplex roll down the ramp out of their spaceship. Their square yellow toes slide into the green grass of the lawn. They are like identical twins, except that Googol has red wrist blocks and Googolplex has blue ones. So it is easy to tell them apart.

"Googol! Googolplex!"

Troy and Pippa jump out of the pool and run toward their friends. Googol and Googolplex bleep and blurp happily when they each get a hug.

"Hello, wet humans. How are you doing?"

Pippa laughs. "I guess we're a bit soggy."

"Never mind us," Troy says. "How are you guys? You've been gone for ages."

Googol bleeps sadly. "Yes, we were given another job to do. We have to count all the moons in your solar system before we can continue our scavenger hunt here on Earth."

"Now that we've counted your moon, we have to fly from planet to planet and count all the others," Googolplex explains.

"No you don't," Pippa says. "I can tell you how many moons there are in our solar system."

"You can?" Googolplex asks.

Pippa nods. "Sure. There are one hundred and forty-one. Our astronomers have counted them all."

Googol's head spins around three times.

"Smart humans!" he says.

"Yes, very smart humans," Googolplex agrees. "Now we can send the answer to our Sunship and continue on our scavenger hunt!"

There are many Sunships moving around the universe like shooting stars. The robots who live on them go on scavenger hunts to study the planets around them.

"That is, if the father-who-is-not-king doesn't mind you helping us," Googol says.

Troy and Pippa smile. The robots used to think that all humans had kings. But all Troy and Pippa have is a father. And right now their father is inside the house trying to find their swimming masks and snorkels. A lot of crashing of drawers and closet doors is going on inside the Sinclair's house.

"I don't think he'll mind," Troy says.

Mr. Sinclair thinks the robots are just pretend. Only Troy and Pippa have seen them. They think that it is safer for Googol and Googolplex to stay a secret.

"Let's tell him we're going to Madame Myfanwy's. She needs some help putting in a new light bulb, and I left something there that I need," Pippa says.

Googolplex's head spins around three times. "Isn't Madame Myfanwy one of those adults who is scared of talking robots and spaceships from outer space?"

"Yes, won't she scream and lock us in her basement?" Googol asks.

Troy laughs. "Nothing scares Madame Myfanwy. I think it's because she's so old."

Pippa nods. "She talks to ghosts!"

"You'll see," Troy says.

Troy and Pippa rush into their house to put on dry clothes.

Mr. Sinclair is happy to let them go over to see Madame Myfanwy.

"Look both ways before you cross the road," he tells them as he settles down in an armchair with a good book.

"Yes, Dad," Pippa and Troy say.

Then they fly across the road in Googol and Googolplex's spaceship.

Chapter Two
Madame Myfanwy

Madame Myfanwy's house is right across from Troy and Pippa's house. There are lots of trees around it, and her backyard goes all the way out to meet the Pacific Ocean.

Googol and Googolplex land their invisible spaceship on Madame Myfanwy's back lawn. Their eyes brighten. The poppies around the house are as red as their square heads. The glimmer of ocean through the trees is as blue as their square shoulders.

"This is a very nice place," Googol says.

"A very nice place," Googolplex says.

Pippa nods. "We're lucky. Madame Myfanwy lets us come over to play here whenever we want to."

Troy rummages through his pockets.

"Oh, no," Troy says. "I forgot the scavenger list you gave us last time!"

There is a whirring sound inside of Googol. A bunch of lights flash on his stomach, and a long piece of paper slides out of his mouth.

Pippa grabs the list and begins to read.

"Six snowballs, four sand dollars, a tutu, the song of a blackbird, two peacock feathers, a chocolate bar, all the colors of a rainbow…"

"Well, you've already got the snowballs, the song of the blackbird and the chocolate bar," Troy says.

"And soon they'll have a tutu," Pippa says.

She runs out of the spaceship and into a small playhouse next to Madame Myfanwy's house. When she comes back she is wearing a frilly pink tutu.

Troy and the robots join Pippa on the lawn as she does a pirouette.

"It's too tight for me now," Pippa tells them. "You can have it if you want."

Pippa slips the tutu over Googolplex's head and down to his middle.

"Go on. Try it out," Pippa says.

Troy laughs as Googolplex puts up his arms and tries to stand on tiptoe. The robot's square toes stick in the lawn.

They hear a tap, tap, tap behind them. Madame Myfanwy comes out through the back door of her house. Her back is as straight as the silver-tipped walking stick in her hand. She was once a great ballerina.

"Not like that! Not like that! You must master the basics. Let me see you put your feet in first position."

Madame Myfanwy walks over to them and points at Googolplex's feet with her stick.

Googolplex stands up straight with his feet wide open like he usually does.

Madame Myfanwy squints at Googolplex's feet. Then she smiles. "Wonderful turn-out, my dear. Just wonderful. You must join my ballet school."

All the lights on Googolplex's body flash in alarm.

"I think I'd be better at a square dance than a round one," Googolplex squeaks.

Madame Myfanwy looks at Pippa and Troy.

"Have you come to help me with my light bulb, children?" she asks. "I can't quite manage it with these fingers of mine."

Madame Myfanwy holds up her knobby fingers. She has arthritis. "You can bring your friends along if you like."

Madame Myfanwy leads them into her house.

Troy stops to whisper to the robots. "See. What did I tell you? She hasn't even noticed that you're robots."

"Come along," Madame Myfanwy calls back to them. "No lollygagging. I have things to do!"

Madame Myfanwy leads them through her dark and dusty house into the kitchen. This room is clean and cozy.

Madame Myfanwy stops beneath the ceiling lamp.

"Do you think that you could reach it from a kitchen chair?" Madame Myfanwy asks Troy.

Troy looks up and frowns. He thinks this might be a job for his father.

Googol rolls forward. "Let me do it for you, Madame."

He picks up the screwdriver that is sitting on the kitchen table. The coiled springs in his legs stretch way out to make him ten feet tall. He unscrews the light cover, puts in the light bulb and replaces the light cover.

Mrs. Myfanwy looks over her shoulder. "Did you see that, Frederick? One of your inventions couldn't have done better, my dear."

Pippa leans over and whispers to Googolplex, "Frederick was her husband. He died five years ago."

Mrs. Myfanwy smiles at Googol when he collapses to his regular size. "Are there many like you two around?"

"Uh, not around here," Troy answers quickly. "They come from far away."

"Pity," Madame Myfanwy says. "You'd be very useful. This house has so many dusty, hard to reach corners."

Madame Myfanwy switches on the overhead light and smiles.

"Never mind. Off you go," she tells them. "I can see that you all want to be on your way. We'll save the tea and cookies for next time, shall we?"

"Yes, please, Madame," Pippa says. "We have to help Googol and Googolplex with their scavenger hunt this morning."

"Oooh, a scavenger hunt," Madame Myfanwy exclaims. She rubs her hands together. "Those are loads of fun! What is the next item on the list?"

"Four sand dollars, I think," Troy says as he pulls out the list.

Madame Myfanwy laughs. "Well, you won't have far to go for those, will you?"

19

She pushes the curtains aside on the kitchen window. The ocean sparkles in the distance. "Just watch out for that Martin Kelly boy, will you? He was down on the beach earlier. He's always up to no good."

Chapter Three
Peacock Feathers

Martin Kelly lives right next door to Troy and Pippa. He is two years older than Troy, and he is a nuisance. The first time Googol and Googolplex came to earth, Martin accidentally saw one of them. They had some real adventures hiding from Martin after that.

"Maybe we should get the peacock feathers first," Pippa says. "We don't want to bump into Martin Kelly."

They all think this is a good idea.

"But where can we find peacock feathers?" Googolplex asks.

"On the Island of Palawan in the Philippines," Troy tells them. "I studied Palawan peacocks at school last year."

They look up the Philippines in an atlas they borrow from Madame Myfanwy. Then they go into Googol and Googolplex's spaceship and look at a wall-sized picture of Earth. Troy points at a clump of islands in the South China Sea.

"That's it!" he says. "And there is the Island of Palawan."

Googol's head spins around three times when he sees it.

"Perfect!" he says.

"Oh, I like this thing called an atlas," Googolplex says. "We'll have to make one for ourselves."

"That's a good idea," Googol says. "But first we must find peacock feathers."

The Island of Palawan is on the other side of Earth, but the robots' spaceship gets them there in only a few minutes.

"Look!" Googol says as they fly over a small group of islands.

"That's them," Troy says. "And the long, skinny one on the left is the Island of Palawan."

They drop down closer to have a look. It is a green, forested island with few houses on it. They land on a grassy hill in the middle of the forest. When they step out of the spaceship, they can hear a lot of different bird songs, but they don't hear a peacock's loud cry.

"I think it might be very hard to find a peacock on an island this big," Pippa says.

"Whew! And it's so hot!" Troy wipes his forehead. "We'd better get out of the sun before we get sunburned."

The robots roll along behind them toward the trees.

"Poor humans," Googolplex says. "Your soft pink bodies don't do well at hot or cold temperatures."

"No," Pippa grumbles as she smacks a buzzing insect off of her arm. "And they don't do well against insect bites either!"

"Or snake bites!" Troy says.

He points to a small green and yellow snake hanging from a tree branch.

"Oooh! I think I want to go home now!" Pippa says.

Googol rolls right up to the snake. The snake flicks its pink tongue at him. Googol's head spins around three times.

"It's really very nice," Googol says.

"Yes," Troy says. He likes snakes. "But tropical snake bites can be poisonous to humans."

"Oh dear," says Googolplex. "Then we shouldn't stay here. The father-who-is-not-king will be very unhappy if we let you get hurt."

As they step back into the hot sun, they hear a loud bird call.

Troy looks at Pippa and Pippa looks at Troy.

"That sounded just like the peacocks at the petting zoo," Pippa says.

In the middle of the long grass, a couple of dark heads are bobbing along. They are heading toward the forest edge.

A peahen and a peacock step out of the grass. One of them looks like a small, dark chicken. The other one has a big tail that opens like a Chinese fan. Many beautiful shiny blue circles, like eyes, decorate his tail.

All the lights on the robots' bodies flash with excitement.

"Oh! Peacocks are beautiful!" Googolplex says.

"Very beautiful!" Googol says.

"That's why people collect their feathers," Pippa says. "Let's hope he's dropped some."

The peacock and the peahen disappear into the forest. Pippa and Troy run up to where the birds were standing. Pippa thinks she can see

something blue and sparkling in the long grass. But she also thinks she can hear voices in the forest.

Googolplex's head spins around three times. "People!"

They stand still and listen. The voices get louder.

"Hurry!" Troy says. "Back to the spaceship!"

Googol and Googolplex lead the way. The spaceship door snaps shut behind Troy and Pippa just as six people hike out of the forest.

"Whew! That was lucky!" Troy says, as the spaceship lifts off. The hikers pass right below them.

But Pippa doesn't think it was lucky at all. The hikers' big feet have trampled right over the peacocks' trail. Pippa can no longer see any sign of sparkly blue feathers lying in the long grass.

Chapter Four
Spring Cleaning

Madame Myfanwy is standing on her back porch when they get back. Pippa and Troy jump out the back of the invisible spaceship and run up toward her.

"Oh, there you are," she exclaims. She squints hard at the spot on her lawn where they magically appeared. "Your father called and asked me to send you home. So, off you go."

"We'll be back tomorrow, Madame," Pippa tells her.

As soon as they finish brushing their teeth and making their beds the next morning, Pippa and Troy rush across to Madame Myfanwy's.

"That's strange," Troy says when he sees Madame Myfanwy's back door standing open.

"Hello?" Pippa calls into the house. Nobody answers.

They peek into the dark, dusty rooms on either side of the hallway. But the rooms are no longer dark and dusty. All the lights are on, and every room is bright and clean.

"Where are all of Madame's paintings?" Pippa asks.

The walls in each room are bare. Rectangles of dark paint show where paintings used to hang.

Troy frowns. "I don't know, Pippa, but I've never heard of a thief who cleans the house while he steals the paintings."

They hear a couple of loud thumps above them. Troy looks at Pippa.

"Come on," Troy says.

They follow the bumps and thumps to a narrow staircase on the second floor.

When they climb these, they find themselves in a large attic.

Googolplex is rolling around upside down. His super-retractable, self-adhesive wheels keep him attached to the sloped ceiling. He is vacuuming up all the cobwebs in hard to reach places with a tiny dust-buster.

Googol is helping Madame Myfanwy stack some paintings against a wall.

"Oh, children!" Madame Myfanwy exclaims as Troy and Pippa's heads pop up into the attic. "You did give me a fright!"

Troy and Pippa roll their eyes.

"That makes us even," Troy says. "What are you all up to?"

"Spring cleaning!" Madame Myfanwy says with a smile.

"We've been helping Madame get rid of all her cobwebs," Googol says.

Googolplex rolls down from the ceiling.

"I can see that," Pippa says with a smile. She pulls a cobweb off of Googolplex's nose.

"And I'm doing a little scavenger hunting too," Madame Myfanwy says.

She steps between all the boxes on the floor and stops in front of a large trunk. When she opens the lid, a puff of satin, tissue and silk spills out.

"I've given away a great many of my old ballet costumes," she says. "But a few of them have remained here, in the attic."

Madame Myfanwy pulls out a silver crown decorated with three peacock feathers. The crown is bent and the silver peeling, but the peacock feathers are perfect.

Madame Myfanwy takes the feathers off the crown and hands them to the robots. "I hope these will do."

The robots' heads spin around three times.

"Perfect!" Googol says, his pale blue eyes glowing warmly.

"Perfect," Googolplex says.

Pippa hugs Madame Myfanwy. "Thank-you, Madame!"

"Now, now. Don't fuss. It's only a few feathers," Madame Myfanwy says.

Troy laughs. "You wouldn't happen to have some sand dollars in there too?"

Madame Myfanwy sniffs. "Don't get lazy, my boy. You only have to walk as far as the beach to find those. Just pick up those young feet of yours and get on with it."

Chapter Five
Sand Dollars and Sand Castles

Troy and Pippa lead the way down to the beach. They look from side to side. The little bay in front of Madame Myfanwy's house is usually quiet. The public beach is just around the corner. There are lots of people on that beach.

Troy shakes his head. "I can't see anyone. Can you, Pippa?"

Pippa shakes her head. "No one."

"It's all clear," they call to the robots.

Googol and Googolplex roll out from between the trees. When they reach the soft sand, their wheels spin around and around, and the robots stop moving.

"Oh, dear," Googol says. His head spins around three times.

"Dear, me," Googolplex says. "I think we'll have to retract our super-retractable, self-adhesive wheels."

Pippa laughs. "Yes, but not for long. The sand out by the ocean is nice and hard."

"And great for making sand castles!" Troy adds. "We're lucky the tide is out."

"Tide? What is this tide?" Googolplex asks.

"It's how high or how low the sea is," Troy tells them.

"When the tide is high," Pippa says, "the ocean comes all the way up to where we are standing now."

"When the tide is low, the edge of the ocean is somewhere out there," Troy says, pointing to the beach. "And we get sandbars. That's where sand dollars live."

Googol and Googolplex beep excitedly.

"Then that is where we will go!" Googolplex says.

The robots retract their wheels. They take small robot steps through the soft sand onto the sandbars. Their feet leave lovely square footprints in the wet sand. They are almost sorry to put their wheels back down again.

Pippa points out the sand dollars in the sand as they near the ocean.

"The black ones are alive. They have to stay here. But these gray and white ones are the skeletons of dead ones."

Pippa picks up a lovely gray and white sand dollar. It is sort of round and there are lines on it that look like a flower. It fits perfectly into Pippa's hand.

"They are very nice," Googol says. He picks one up out of the sand, and Googolplex finds a couple more.

"I'll go get our buckets to carry them in," Troy says.

He runs back to the bottom of Madame Myfanwy's yard. When he comes back, he is carrying two

shovels and two buckets. One of the buckets is round and yellow and the other one is square and red.

Googol and Googolplex put their sand dollars in the round bucket.

"Perfect," says Googolplex.

"Perfect," says Googol. "Now, what can we put in this red bucket?"

"Sand," Pippa says.

She points along the sandbar to a castle someone else has built.

"That's an ordinary sand castle," Pippa says. "I think we should make something a little different."

Googol and Googolplex help Troy and Pippa fill the bucket many times. Each time, Pippa empties it carefully onto the sandbar. After a while they can all see a square-headed robot lying on the sand. They use rocks and shells to make eyes and lights. Then they are done.

Troy grins. "A sand robot!"

Googolplex's head spins around. "Can we make another one?"

Pippa laughs. "I don't think me have time. Look. The tide's coming in."

And sure enough, the ocean is creeping in around them. Their sandbar is getting smaller and smaller.

Googolplex gives a series of alarmed beeps and squeaks. "The sand robot will be washed away!"

"I'm afraid so," Troy says. "But we have bigger problems than that."

He points to the trail that leads to the beach beside Mrs. Myfanwy's house. Martin Kelly is heading toward them.

"Quick, hide!" Troy tells the robots.

A couple of huge rocks are halfburied in the sandbar. Googol and Googolplex crouch behind these.

Pippa and Troy gather up their shovels and pails and head up the beach.

"Hi, Martin," Troy says, when they reach him.

"You better not have wrecked my castle or I'll stomp on yours!" Martin Kelly tells them.

Troy rolls his eyes. "It's too late, Martin. The ocean is wrecking both of them."

Sure enough, the ocean has closed in over the sandbar. Their sand robot and Martin's castle are collapsing under the waves.

"Darn! I was going to catch a couple of fish to put in the moat," Martin says. "Maybe I'll just go swimming instead."

Just then, Mr. Sinclair appears at the bottom of Madame Myfanwy's property. "Troy! Pippa!" he calls. "Lunch is ready!"

Martin laughs. "Hurry along, now, kiddies. Your daddy's calling."

Pippa and Troy run up the beach to their father.

"Oooh! That Martin Kelly!" Pippa says as she runs. "We have to get him away from here before he finds Googol and Googolplex."

"Don't worry, Pippa," Troy says. "He'll head to the public beach to swim. He only hangs around here to bother us. But we better eat our lunch as fast as we can. Googol and Googolplex must be knee-deep in water by now, and I doubt they can swim."

Chapter Six
Fish-Robots

Googol and Googolplex lean on the big rocks in front of them. They bleep and blurp in alarm as Troy and Pippa leave the beach with their father.

"Oh, dear! They are leaving us alone with Martin Kelly!" Googolplex says.

"And in all this deep water!" Googol says.

But Martin Kelly doesn't stay. He heads around the corner of the bay to the public beach, just like Troy said he would. By that time, the ocean has reached the top of the robots' legs.

A big wave wobbles them from side to side.

"Oh, dear!" Googol says. "I wish we'd asked Troy and Pippa what humans do when the tide comes in."

The next big wave tips Googol face-first into the water. But he doesn't sink. The air in his body makes him float.

Googol turns his face to the sky. "Look, Googolplex! I'm a fish-robot!"

Googol turns his wheels forward and backward. He moves in the water like a small motor boat.

Soon, Googol is heading out to sea.

"Come back, come back!" Googolplex calls.

Googolplex's head spins around three times. Then a wave knocks him into the ocean and he floats too.

"Oh, dear!" Googolplex cries. Then he starts chugging through the water just like Googol. "This is fun!"

Googol and Googolplex go up and down the beach. They stare down at the fish swimming under them. They stare up at the sea birds flying above them.

"Look!" Googol says, his square red head bobbing up and down in the water.

Googol points at all the people swimming at the public beach.

"Humans can move in the water too!" Googolplex says.

Martin Kelly is one of the people in the water. He is playing with two little boys. The boys have an air mattress to lie on. Martin keeps flipping the little boys into the water. Then he steals their mattress and heads into deep water. "That Martin Kelly!" Googol says.

"He is causing trouble again," Googolplex says.

"We better not let him see us," Googol says.

Googol and Googolplex spin their wheels really fast and dive to the floor of the ocean. Soon they are motoring along underneath Martin Kelly.

Googol and Googolplex avoid the kelp that grows like slippery brown ribbons beneath the surface of the ocean. But Martin does not see the kelp. The brown ribbons turn and twist around his kicking feet.

"Ahhhh!" Martin yells. "Sharks!"

Googol and Googolplex pull the kelp away from Martin's feet.

Martin tucks his feet under him on the air mattress and paddles furiously toward shore with his hands. Soon he reaches the little boys. They take back their air mattress, and Martin runs for shore.

"Sharks, sharks!" Martin yells. "Run for it!"

But the only one running is Martin. The other people on the beach shake their heads and go back to swimming and sunbathing.

"Perfect!" Googol says as his head bobs above the surface of the ocean.

"Perfect!" Googolplex says. "Now maybe that Martin Kelly will go home."

The robots follow along in the sea as Martin runs along the shore. Soon they are all back in front of Madame Myfanwy's house.

Martin slows down and kicks at rocks and seashells. When he sees Pippa and Troy's red and yellow buckets sitting on a log, he walks over and kicks them too. Their sand dollars go flying.

"Our beautiful sand dollars!" Googol says.

"Troy and Pippa's beautiful buckets!" Googolplex says.

Googol and Googolplex wait until Martin is gone. Then they roll up the beach and rescue Troy and Pippa's buckets. Googol's eyes brighten. "The buckets are unharmed."

Googolplex bleeps sadly. "The sand dollars are not."

Their sand dollars are lying in pieces between the logs.

"What are we going to do?" Googolplex asks.

Googol's head spins around three times.

"We are going to find more sand dollars!" Googol says. "And we're going to do it before Pippa and Troy get back! Come on."

Googolplex follows Googol back down to the ocean. They roll into the water and in a few moments they disappear from sight.

Chapter Seven
Under the Sea

The first thing Pippa and Troy see when they come back to the beach is their red and yellow buckets bobbing up and down in the water.

"What are our buckets doing way out there?" Troy asks. Pippa shakes her head. "I don't know, Troy. But it's a good thing we changed into our bathing suits."

They look around for Googol and Googolplex.

Pippa bites her bottom lip.

"Do you think they sank to the bottom of the ocean?" she asks.

Troy shakes his head. "I don't know, but I'm glad we found our masks and snorkels. Come on!"

Pippa and Troy put on their masks and snorkels and jump into the ocean. They swim out and stand on the rocks where Googol and Googolplex were hiding. They cannot see the robots anywhere.

Troy walks over to the floating buckets. "Look at this, Pippa," he says.

They both look down into the round, yellow bucket. There are two nice white sand dollars inside.

"I wonder what happened to the other two," Pippa says.

Just then, Googol and Googolplex's square red heads burst through the surface of the ocean.

Pippa and Troy jump back in surprise.

Googol and Googolplex beep in alarm. They don't recognize Pippa and Troy with their masks and snorkels on.

"Googol!" Pippa cries out happily.

"Googolplex!" Troy says. He laughs. "You can swim!"

Pippa and Troy push up their masks. The robots stop beeping.

"We are fish-robots," Googolplex says. "Watch."

He lies on his back on top of the water and makes himself go forward and then back again.

Troy laughs. "Actually, I think you are ro-boats."

Googol lifts his hand out of the water. He is holding another nice sand dollar. So is Googolplex.

"But what happened to the ones we collected earlier?" Pippa asks.

Googol and Googolplex drop their sand dollars into the square, red bucket. Then they look at Pippa and Troy.

"That is a long story," they say.

Troy frowns. "It doesn't involve Martin Kelly, does it?"

"I am afraid it does," Googol says.

"You are a very smart human," Googolplex says. "But Martin Kelly is not."

The robots explain what happened. Troy and

Pippa laugh when they hear about Martin and the sharks. They stop laughing when the robots tell them about Martin kicking their buckets.

"He could have broken them!" Troy says angrily.

"Yes, but he did not," Googol says. "And we have found four new sand dollars."

"So, now you can show us what swimming is," Googolplex says.

Pippa and Troy show them the breaststroke and the crawl. Then they all do somersaults and handstands. Pippa and Troy keep popping back to the surface for air. But the robots stay under the water the whole time.

Finally, they swim into shallow water. Pippa and Troy sit on the sand with their knees up. They are tired.

"You are lucky humans," Googolplex tells them. "You swim like fish. You are very flexible."

"But we can't stay underwater forever, like you can," Troy says. "And we get tired."

Pippa sighs. "I bet you could swim to China if you wanted."

Googolplex's head spins around three times. "I do not think we would want to. I think we would run out of energy."

"And then we would be stuck in the middle of the ocean," Googol says.

"Human bodies may not be perfect," Googolplex says. "But robot bodies can't make their own energy."

"Tomorrow we will have to go back to our Sunship to recharge our solar-powered spaceship," Googol says.

"Already?" Pippa asks.

"Yes," Googol answers. "We have used up a lot of energy swimming. But we have one more day to spend on Earth. You must help us use it well."

Chapter Eight
A Good Last Day

"You two are very quiet this evening," Mr. Sinclair tells his children.

Pippa and Troy have hardly spoken during dinner. They are thinking of the next item on Googol and Googolplex's scavenger list. They are wondering how they can help them find it. And they are sad because the robots will be leaving soon.

"You didn't have any trouble down on the beach, did you?" Mr. Sinclair asks. "I was cleaning the front windows when Martin came back from having a swim. He was telling his mother a story about sharks nibbling at his toes."

Pippa and Troy giggle into their hands.

Mr. Sinclair sighs. "Yes, I know. That boy does come up with the most incredible stories. Last month it was robots, now it's sharks. He must drive his parents crazy."

Mr. Sinclair begins clearing the table. Pippa and Troy get up to put their own plates and cutlery into the dishwasher.

"Madame Myfanwy is trying to find someone to do some painting in her house," Mr. Sinclair says. "Why don't we all go over and help her tomorrow? You can take a break from being beach bums."

"Oh, not tomorrow!" Pippa says.

"There aren't any sharks in our ocean, Dad! Honest!" Troy says.

Mr. Sinclair smiles and ruffles his children's hair. "I know, I know. But Madame Myfanwy is like a grandmother to you guys. And if she needs our help, I think we have to make sure to offer it to her."

Of course, Mr. Sinclair is right. But Pippa and Troy have trouble remembering that when they are knocking on Madame Myfanwy's back door the next morning. All they can think about is Googol and Googolplex.

They look back at the spot where the robots have been parking their spaceship.

"They're probably sitting in their spaceship watching us right now," Troy whispers in Pippa's ear.

"Good morning," Madame Myfanwy says. "Well, you three certainly look dressed for the job."

They are wearing old blue jeans and big messy paint shirts.

Madame Myfanwy motions toward a large parlor just past the back door. "I thought you and I could start in here, Mr. Sinclair. I have two other painters working upstairs in the guest bedrooms. The children can go and help them if they like."

Pippa and Troy head slowly toward the staircase.

Madame Myfanwy shoos them along with a wave of her hand.

"Don't drag your feet, children. Time is precious," she says.

"That's for sure," Troy mumbles.

Pippa and Troy would give almost anything to see Googol and Googolplex once more before they leave. They hurry into the second-story bedroom where they can hear the painters working. They hope they will be able to catch sight of Googol and Googolplex from the windows in this room. But what they find is ... Googol and Googolplex!

The robots are wearing men's dress shirts that reach past their toes. Polka-dotted, red kerchiefs cover their square heads. And they both have paint rollers in their hands.

Troy laughs. "Don't tell me you guys have been put to work too?"

"You should be spending your last day on Earth having fun, not doing chores," Pippa says.

Googolplex's head spins around three times.

"What are chores?" he asks.

"Dusting, vacuuming, fixing things," Troy says. "Things that humans do only because they have to."

"But dusting hard to reach places is fun," Googolplex says.

"And painting is fun," Googol says.

Googol tips sideways and rolls up a wall to the ceiling. Then he paints a nice, straight line along the top of the wall.

Googolplex stretches the coiled springs in his legs as he paints a straight line all the way down the corner of one wall.

Pippa and Troy shake their heads.

"Well, you certainly make it look like fun," Pippa says.

She borrows Googolplex's paint roller. She makes a wobbly line up the wall next to Googolplex's line. When she has reached as high as she can, Googolplex picks her up. He stretches up and up and up until Pippa has painted all the way to the top of the nine-foot wall.

Googol gives Troy his own paint roller. He tells Troy to sit on the tops of his yellow toes. Troy sits down and presses the paint roller against the wall. When Googol rolls forward, Troy makes a neat line of paint from one corner of the wall to another.

Troy grins and Googol's eyes glow.

"You see," Googol says. "Painting is fun."

It is. Pippa and Troy even enjoy painting places that they can reach all by themselves. And, when they are tired, they enjoy standing by the door watching Googol and Googolplex paint.

"Perfect!" Googol says as he finishes painting one wall.

"Perfect!" Googolplex says as he finishes the opposite wall.

Troy and Pippa smile. They have, after all, found a good way to spend the last day of Googol and Googolplex's visit.

Next time the robots come to Earth they will continue their scavenger hunt. Today they will make Madame Myfanwy's beautiful old house look like new again. They know that the look of happiness on Madame Myfanwy's face will be as wonderful as all the colors in a rainbow.

Nelly Kazenbroot loved to collect sand dollars when she was growing up. Now she loves to write. She based Googol and Googolplex on small Lego characters that she created years ago. Nelly lives in Nanaimo, British Columbia with her family.

Nelly Kazenbroot created the interior illustrations for *Under the Sea with Googol and Googolplex* in pencil. **Laura Watson** created the cover illustration in acrylic. Laura lives in Toronto with her husband.

Down the Chimney with Googol and Googolplex

1-55143-290-0 • $6.95 CDN • $4.99 US